BOOKASURA

THE ADVENTURES OF BALA AND THE BOOK-EATING MONSTER

Arundhati Venkatesh

Illustrated by Priya Kuriyan

SCHOLASTIC
New York Toronto London Auckland
Sydney New Delhi Hong Kong

For the little monster at home who devours books
by the dozen
And for booklovers everywhere.

Copyright © 2014 Arundhati Venkatesh
Illustrations © 2014 Priya Kuriyan

Published by Scholastic India Pvt. Ltd.
A subsidiary of Scholastic Inc., New York, 10012 (USA).
Publishers since 1920, with international operations in Canada,
Australia, New Zealand, the United Kingdom, India, and Hong Kong.

For information regarding permission, write to:
Scholastic India Pvt. Ltd.
A-27, Ground Floor, Bharti Sigma Centre
Infocity-1, Sector 34, Gurgaon 122001 (India)

First edition: December 2014 May *2015*

ISBN-13: 978-93-5103-706-4

Printed at: Ram Printograph, Delhi

Contents

Contents

Summer Holidays Begin

'Amma! Look! I read a chapter book. It has more than a HUNDRED pages!' <u>Bala</u> <u>burst</u> out as he entered the room.

'Shhhh! Baby's feeding,' Amma shushed him.

That's how it always was these days. Amma was forever busy with the baby. Baby was either eating, or sleeping, or making silly sounds. She was nct to be disturbed.

Bala waited for Amma to finish. He thought about the book he had just read—*Moin and the Monster*. The monster in the book did nothing but eat bananas or sing silly songs. Not very different from his baby sister! For a minute, he imagined the baby growing into a monster. Bala shuddered at the thought.

Amma was finally done feeding the baby.

'Amma, it says here there is another book— *Moin the Monster Songster*. Can you get it for me?'

'We'll see,' Amma replied. 'I have to get Baby to burp now. If she doesn't, she'll throw up all that she's eaten.'

Bala sighed. He was quite sure Amma hadn't even heard what he'd said. Feed the baby, burp the baby, bathe the baby, baby this, baby that. It was always about Baby. It was as if Bala didn't even exist.

It was a good thing Bala had books. He sat down to read another one. The cover said brave

Tashi was too clever for giants and demons. Bala decided it would be useful to know how one went about <u>outwitting</u> monsters. Just in case he ever encountered one.

Bala was engrossed in Tashi's adventures when Appa came into the room.

He went straight towards Baby to pinch her cheeks. Bala watched as Amma mouthed 'NO'.

'I've washed my hands,' Appa insisted.

Amma pointed towards the baby. She was

asleep. So *that's* why Appa wasn't allowed to pinch her cheeks. Bala's parents tiptoed out of the room. They shut the door after them.

Bala could hear their voices faintly. It seemed like they were discussing something important, something they did not want him to hear.

Bala walked quietly towards the closed door. He peered through the keyhole—they were talking animatedly.

He put his ear to the door—he could hear them better that way.

'What will he do here all day? You don't have the time. Neither do I. It's different when he has school,' Appa was saying.

Hmm. They were talking about him. And they didn't want him to hear. Bala listened intently.

'He is still so young. How can he go all alone?' Amma argued.

'Navaneeth and Kala are taking the bus to Melagam tomorrow. He won't have to travel alone,' Appa replied.

'With Kala? You know how she is!' Amma protested.

'It's only a few hours,' Appa said.

So they were planning to send him off to his grandparents at Melagam. He would have to spend the rest of the summer holidays there.

Bala saw the figures move. They were coming towards him! He scampered away from the door.

The Book-eating Baby

Just in time!

Bala reached out for the book. Hey! Where was it? He'd left it right there, but it was missing now. Where could it have gone?

Just then he heard the baby gurgling. So she was awake. Wait! She had his book! 'AMMA! She has my book,' he screamed in horror.

Amma took one look at the scene and started gushing happily. 'I always knew she was smart. See, she's into books already!'

Amma thought she was a genius, a prodigy, reading books as an infant!

A closer look revealed that the cause of the

cooing was the taste of paper—a couple of pages from the book were missing! A few pieces were still sticking to Baby's teeth—she had only four of them, right in front, like fangs.

'My book, my book,' Bala howled.

But Amma was only concerned about the baby, not about Bala's book. 'O my baby! Don't worry, we'll get everything out,' she rushed with Baby to the bathroom and sent Appa off to the kitchen to get some water.

That was it; Bala decided he would be better off at his grandparents' house. He would have to keep his books under lock and key, otherwise the baby would eat them all up in his absence.

Bala arranged all his books in the cupboard. Then he locked it up. His books were safe.

But what was he to do? Bala was bored without his books. He looked around. He saw the TV and switched it on.

By then Amma and Appa had finished fussing over the baby.

'Bala! You're watching TV!' Amma sounded horrified.

'I can't read. All my books are locked inside,' Bala said.

Amma went on about how the rays from TV attacked the eyes, the brain and the imagination. TV seemed like a powerful weapon!

'There's something we have to tell you,' Appa announced when Amma stopped for breath.

Bala knew what was coming.

'Amma and I felt you would have more fun at Melagam with your grandparents,' Appa hesitated. 'Navaneeth uncle and Kala aunty are returning to

their home in Melagam. So they will be travelling by the same bus as you.'

Bala nodded.

Appa seemed surprised by his reaction. 'You're not upset?'

'I can't even read in peace here,' Bala shrugged and pointed towards the room where Baby was asleep ... supposedly. Who knew what she was *really* up to? 'I'll take ten books,' Bala continued.

'Ten? That's too many. Your bag will be too full and too heavy. How will you carry your clothes and the rest of your things then?'

'I'll take ten *thin* books,' Bala said.

So Bala chose exactly ten books to take with him to Melagam, along with his clothes and things. He left the rest of his books in the cupboard, locked up. He was ready for the trip.

Melagam

Bala boarded the bus with the bag of books.

Conductor Velu ruffled his hair and put his bag up on the rack. Bala thanked him and paid for his ticket. 'I hear you're a big brother now. I get to know things on the bus, you know?' Velu uncle said. Bala smiled politely and took his seat near the window.

Bala saw Navaneeth uncle and Kala aunty getting on the bus. Navaneeth uncle and Appa had been best friends for the longest time. Kala aunty and Navaneeth uncle sat beside him. 'Who does the baby look like?' was Kala aunty's first question. Why couldn't they talk of anything

else? 'Babies are boring. Let's talk about Bala instead,' Navaneeth uncle winked at Bala. Bala liked Navaneeth uncle.

'We have plenty of mangoes and jackfruit this year. Come with your grandfather. You can eat to your heart's content,' Navaneeth uncle smiled indulgently. Navaneeth uncle's house was called *Thottatthaan*, or house-with-a-garden.

'Mango and jackfruit will cause boils and

blisters ... too much heat,' Kala aunty cautioned.

'Oh, he'll be fine if he has tender-coconut water,' Navaneeth uncle said.

'Do you know how to cut coconuts open? I'll show you how it's done,' Navaneeth uncle promised Bala. 'You can come every day and help out. There's a lot of work to be done. Making compost and using it as manure. I hope you are not queasy about mud and worms like some kids from the city are?' Navaneeth uncle continued.

Bala shook his head.

'There's a fish pond too,' said Navaneeth uncle. 'Needs cleaning,' he added.

This trip was going to be fun.

'Just make sure you don't go near the well,' Kala aunty cautioned.

Bala shook his head again.

He looked out of the window. The temple tower was in sight—it would only be minutes now. The bus slowed down and came to a stop. Bala clambered out and ran to his grandfather.

'He's grown so tall,' Navaneeth uncle said to Bala's grandfather. 'Do bring him home.' Navaneeth uncle waved as he walked away.

Bala and his grandfather walked home. 'Raghu Thaatha, tell me a story,' Bala demanded.

'Not now. Wait till you get home,' said Raghu Thaatha.

'Nooo! Why?' Bala protested.

'Too much traffic,' was Raghu Thaatha's response.

Bala looked around. There were cyclists, flower-sellers and goats.

In a few minutes they had reached home. Ambu Paati was waiting at the gate, beaming at him. 'How thin you've become!' was her first comment. She always said that. 'We'll fatten you up in three weeks,' she assured him. Feeding and fattening people was Ambu Paati's pet project. Bala didn't mind!

'Take a bath, you've come by bus,' Ambu Paati shooed him off.

'What will you eat? There's *pongal, vada, idli, dosa, chutney* and *sambar*. I've made all your favourites,' she said when he had bathed.

'Everything!' Bala grinned.

Ambu Paati was pleased. She watched while Bala ate, serving him second and third helpings of everything.

'Here, have some *mysore pak*,' she said when he was done.

Bala had no space left in his tummy, but how could he refuse *mysore pak*?! So he ate a piece. Mmɪn! It tasted so good Bala *had* to have another. Paati offered him yet another piece. Bala was about to explode by this time, but he agreed to have half of it.

Bala was so full, he couldn't move. It was only then that he remembered Raghu Thaatha's promise to tell him a story once they got home. He curled up on the big swing like a python, 'Thaatha, tell me a story!'

'Your Paati has fed you as if you are Bakasura,' Raghu Thaatha remarked.

'What is that?'

'Who, not what,' Raghu Thaatha corrected. 'Bakasura was a demon Bhima defeated.'

'Tell me the story of Bakasura,' Bala said immediately.

Raghu Thaatha had told him lots of stories from the Ramayana and Mahabharata, about Krishna and Hanuman, Kalidasa's tales, stories of the Greek hero Ulysses, but Bala had not heard the story of Bakasura before.

Bakasura

Raghu Thaatha settled down beside Bala on the swing. Bala sat up, listening.

Thaatha began the story, *'Long ago, many thousands of years ago, in the time of the Mahabharata, there lived a gigantic demon named Bakasura. Bakasura lived in a cave in the hills surrounding a place called Ekachakra. Now, this demon was humungous, so he needed enormous quantities of food to eat. He plundered villages, looted their crops and ate their cattle up to satisfy his hunger. Men, women and children were not spared either. The people there were a very troubled lot. They did not know what to do. But they had a wise leader. The* leader came up with a plan. "We will send you a cartload of the finest food everyday; you will not have to bother to come down to the village," he said to Bakasura. The plan suited Bakasura, so he agreed. Bakasura ate the food, the bullocks that drew the cart, and the person who drove it. Still, it was better than the entire village being ransacked and children being devoured. The cart went from a different family each day. The headman decided whose turn it was. So, every day, one family in the village cooked a feast for Bakasura, loaded it all on a bullock cart and bade goodbye to someone from the family. Neither the bullocks nor the person would return.'

Raghu Thaatha's narration was punctuated by Ambu Paati's rhythmic snoring, 'nnnkkktttrrr nnnkkktttrrr'. Paati turned in her sleep. The snoring stopped.

Thaatha continued with the story, 'It so happened that Kunti and her sons, the five Pandavas, who were in exile, passed by this village. They stopped there and stayed at one of the houses. One day, Kunti saw the lady of the house wiping away her tears.

"What's the matter?" Kunti was concerned.

"I do not want to burden you with my sorrow," said the lady.

When Kunti insisted, the lady broke into tears. She told Kunti about the demon Bakasura and how the villagers had been terrorised until their leader had come up with a solution. Today it was their turn. She had to send her son. She would never get to see him again.

"You have only one son. I have five. Bhima will go instead of your son," said Kunti.

"No! You are our guests. It is our turn ... it is only fair that I send my son," the lady protested.

"Don't worry. Bhima is a mighty warrior. He has slain several demons. He will defeat Bakasura," Kunti assured her.

After much persuasion, the lady agreed. Bhima was to drive the cart with food that she prepared.

Kunti told Bhima about Bakasura and revealed her plan. Bhima got ready to leave.'

'Oh no. Will Bakasura eat Bhima up?' Bala shrieked.

'Shhh,' Ambu Paati waved at Bala with her eyes tightly shut. They were not to disturb her.

Thaatha lowered his voice and went on, *'Mounds of rice, huge vessels with vegetables, baskets full of fruits, and many varieties of sweets were loaded onto the cart. Bhima set off from the village and drove the cart towards the hills. He stopped a little distance away from the cave. He spread all the food around him and sat down to eat. Bhima was ravenous. He ate up the rice and vegetables. Then he finished the fruits and finally the sweets. He let out a very loud belch when he was done. It was so loud that it frightened the birds and beasts of the forest.*

Hearing the cries of the animals, Bakasura came out of his cave to see what the commotion was about. He saw the empty vessels and baskets lying strewn around. There was nothing left for him to eat! Bakasura was furious! Who had dared anger him? His eyes fell on Bhima.

"How dare you eat the food that was sent for me? Do

you not know who I am?" Bakasura boomed.

"The food may have been meant for you, but you were late and I was hungry," Bhima answered.

"You may have eaten my food, but I am going to eat you anyway," Bakasura roared and charged towards Bhima.

But Bhima stood like a wall and Bakasura fell to the ground with a thud. The earth shook as the two giants fought. Bakasura uprooted trees and threw them at Bhima. Bhima caught them and flung them away as if they were twigs. At last, the duel came to an end. Bhima was victorious. Bakasura had been vanquished.

Bhima drove back to the village with Bakasura tied to the cart. The villagers could not believe what they saw. They welcomed Bhima back with great fanfare. "Bakasura has been defeated! Long live Bhima!" the villagers rejoiced.'

'That was the end of Bakasura and this is the end of the story,' said Raghu Thaatha. 'Time for me to sleep now,' he declared.

Bala thought about the story Thaatha had told him and about Bakasura. He wondered what Bakasura looked like. Thaatha hadn't said. Would

he have a moustache? He would definitely have fangs—all demons did.

Bala's thoughts were interrupted by Paati— she had woken up. 'I'm going to make *puri*s, do you want to learn?'

Bala watched as she rolled them out and released them into the oil. Each *puri* puffed up magically. *Puri*s with Paati's potato *masala* ... perfect!

By the time he was done eating, Thaatha was
up. They left for Navaneeth uncle's house.

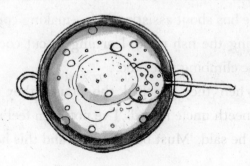

In the Garden

Navaneeth uncle's house was not too far away. Bala trailed behind Raghu Thaatha, swinging his bag. It had the books he had brought from home. Living with a book-eating baby had made him cautious. He was going to carry his books wherever he went.

Bala recalled what Navaneeth uncle had said on the bus about assisting him—making compost, cleaning the fish pond, learning to cut coconuts, maybe climbing trees too.

When they reached the house, they found Navaneeth uncle in bed. 'I've not been feeling too well,' he said. 'Must be the travel and this heat.'

'Too many mangoes cause trouble in the tummy,' Kala aunty walked in.

'We can't work today,' Navaneeth uncle said apologetically to Bala, 'but you can go around the garden.'

'I'll rest my aching legs  here. Come back before sunset,' Raghu Thaatha sat down to talk to Navaneeth uncle.

'Don't go anywhere near the well,' Kala aunty warned him again.

Bala wandered off.

He looked up at the trees. The jackfruit tree had fruits of all sizes hanging from it. They reminded him of armadillos!

The mango tree was next. He picked up a stone and aimed at a

mango. Two fell! Bala didn't want to put them in his bag. What if the books got stained? He put the mangoes in his pockets.

Ooh! There were so many guava trees and the lemon tree was loaded with yellow and green lemons!

Bala kept walking. He lost track of time. He stepped on dried leaves and listened to them crunch under his chappals. He had his eyes on the trees throughout. He didn't want to miss anything.

Suddenly, he realised there were no trees and

the crackling of leaves had stopped too. He looked around. Where was he? He had reached the big well. Why had Kala aunty asked him not to come here?

He ventured near the well. It was okay, he would be careful not to lean over and fall in.

He could see water far below. He threw a stone and peered in to see the ripples.

Bala was tired; he had walked a long way. He sat down to rest his legs. He began reading one of the books he had brought.

His eyes hurt; he shut them for a moment.

There was a flash in the sky, then a crash.

What he saw made him freeze.

Bookasura

There, before Bala, stood a giant. A giant with many heads. A monster! Was this Ravana? Were there ten heads? Bala was too terrified to count. He just stood there shaking, clutching his bag. Each head had a moustache and fangs. One eye in each head blazed like the sun, the other gleamed like the moon. The eyebrows looked like brooms.

'Who are you? No one has dared venture near my den before,' the monster thundered.

When the monster talked, all the mouths moved.

Bala was too scared to speak. When he opened his mouth, nothing came out.

'Answer me!' the monster sounded even fiercer now.

'*The Boy in the Garden*,' Bala mumbled.

'Don't you have a name?' the monster growled.

'*Gruffalo*,' it came out as a squeak.

'That sounds like a terrifying name for a bite-sized boy! I could easily squeeze you between my fingers!' the monster laughed. 'Where have you come from?'

'*Where the Wild Things Are*,' came Bala's response. He didn't know what he was saying. He was just saying the first thing that came to his mind. They happened to be his favourite books.

'Do you have food? What have you brought? It's been ages since I've eaten anything.'

Bala shook his head. '*No, David!*'

'David? That's not my name. I am Bookasura!' he boomed. 'What on earth did you think I was?'

'*The Pleasant Rakshasa*,' Bala was barely audible.

'What do you have in that bag?' Bookasura barked.

Bala handed the bag over to Bookasura meekly.

'You like them?' Bookasura asked.

Bala nodded, 'I can read with my eyes shut!'

Bookasura smacked his lips. He picked up *I Can Read with My Eyes Shut!* and dropped the bag. He closed his eyes and sniffed at the book. He felt it all over. Then he gobbled it up!

Bala was in tears. His precious book ... gone ... just like that!

Bookasura picked up *No, David!* and popped it into one of his mouths. He munched and chewed with great relish.

He ate up *The Pleasant Rakshasa* next. Bookasura was devouring all of Bala's books!

Bookasura had *The Boy in the Garden* in his hand. Bala remembered the story of Bakasura. He would eat the person carrying the food after he was done eating everything! And Bookasura had said Bala was bite-sized. Bala picked up the bag with the six remaining books, turned tail and dashed! He ran back to the house, crying all the way. 'My books ... my books ...' was all he could say. He was hysterical.

Is Bookasura Real?

Bala had reached the door of the house. There were tears streaming down his face.

He rubbed his face using the sleeve of his shirt. Bala took a deep breath and entered the room.

Navaneeth uncle saw him first. 'You look as if you've seen a ghost!'

'What happened? Are you alright? Your face has gone white and you've been crying,' Raghu Thaatha was concerned.

'I saw something ... near the well. There was a monster ... I was scared,' the words came rushing out.

'I told you not to go near the well,' Kala aunty

glared at him.

'I think we should go now,' Raghu Thaatha said.

Bala held Raghu Thaatha's hand all the way home.

'What happened?' Raghu Thaatha asked after a while.

'I was walking around in the garden. There was a monster near the well,' Bala blurted out.

'Monsters are only in the mind,' Raghu Thaatha said.

'Bookasura ate up my books,' Bala continued.

'Bookasura ... Bakasura ... it is all *bakwaasura*,' Raghu Thaatha chortled.

Bala always enjoyed Thaatha's puns and silly jokes, but today he didn't laugh.

'*Bakwaas* means nonsense in Hindi,' Raghu Thaatha explained. He thought Bala hadn't got the joke.

Bala was quiet.

'Hmm. I shouldn't have told you the story of Bakasura,' Thaatha said. 'It's just a story.'

'Bookasura eats books just like Baby. He looked a lot like Baby too. Do you think Baby ate up all my books and grew into a giant?' Bala asked.

'Meera is just a baby, Bala.'

They walked silently the rest of the way.

As soon as Ambu Paati saw Bala, she panicked. 'You look pale. Do you have a fever?' she touched his forehead.

'He thinks he saw a monster,' Raghu Thaatha told her.

'I don't *think* I saw a monster. I did see a monster!' Bala was indignant.

'Eat this, everything will be alright,' Paati pushed a plate of *murukku* and *jaangiri* towards him. Ambu Paati thought food was the solution to everything.

Bala munched through the crunchy twists of *murukku*. Then he polished off the juicy *jaangiris*.

'The ends of the monster's moustache were curled. Like these *murukkus* and *jaangiris*,' he said when he had finished.

Paati nodded sympathetically.

'The kid has too much of an imagination for his own good,' Raghu Thaatha muttered while taking off his shirt.

'Were the snacks tasty? Was the *murukku* crisp enough? Were the *jaangiris* too sweet?' Paati asked Bala.

Bala tugged at the hair near his ears. He was deep in thought. 'Why did Kala aunty keep warning me not to go near the well? Does she know about the monster?'

Raghu Thaatha raised his eyebrows and looked at Bala questioningly.

'I wandered off and found myself near the well. That's where I saw Bookasura,' Bala explained.

'Bookasura?' asked Ambu Paati.

'That's the monster,' said Bala.

'I shouldn't have told him about Bakasura.' Thaatha was sheepish.

'Why do you tell him stories about demons? Aren't there enough stories about gods? Scaring the poor child!' Paati grumbled.

'It's true, the monster is real,' Bala persisted.

'The child is very smart for his age. Someone has cast the evil eye. So many people must have seen him in the bus today,' Paati had decided to remedy the evil eye. She made a circular motion with her right arm while chanting some mumbo jumbo.

Nobody believed anything Bala said.

Just then the phone rang.

It was Amma. Bala rushed to the phone.

He told her all about Bookasura. Amma listened, she didn't dismiss him.

'Is the baby there? Has she eaten all my books?' Bala was worried.

'Baby is right here, next to me. Your books are safe,' Amma assured him.

Bala heaved a sigh of relief. Nothing had happened to his books. So Bookasura was not the baby. Why did Bookasura resemble her so much? And what did Kala aunty know?

'Here, drink your milk and go to sleep,' Paati handed him a tall glass. 'Don't be afraid, you can sleep with me. No more nightmares,' she said.

'It was not a nightmare.'

Paati looked at Thaatha accusingly. He was to blame for everything.

Bala went to bed by himself.

Bookasura is Back

Bala tossed and turned in bed. He found it impossible to sleep.

The baby, Bookasura, Kala aunty, his books ... the images kept flashing before his eyes.

He tried to make sense of all that had happened. Why didn't anyone believe he had seen a monster? He had seen Bookasura, wasn't it true? It was all very confusing. He felt his eyelids droop.

The bed shook. Bala braced himself. Then he heard it. The flash and the crash, the rumbling of thunder. Bookasura was back!

'Did you think you could escape from my clutches? I will crush you and turn you to dust! I

45

will destroy you!'

'No!' Bala managed to say.

'I am going to eat you, you little vermin. There will be no trace left of you!' Bookasura bared his fangs.

'No ... don't! Don't do that!' Bala remembered the story Raghu Thaatha had told him, the story of Bakasura. He thought of what the villagers had done with Bakasura. He could do something similar with Bookasura!

'If you eat me today, what will you do for the rest of your life? Spare me and I will bring you three scrumptious books every day.'

'A three-course meal every day? For the rest of my life? I will never have to hunt for food?' Bookasura was incredulous.

'Yes ... every single day. I will bring them myself. Where do you live?' Bala asked.

'In the cave near the well,' was Bookasura's response.

Bala nodded. 'Here are the three books for today.' He held out three of his favourite books, *The Gruffalo*, *Where the Wild Things Are* and *Brundibar*.

Bookasura grabbed them. The books disappeared down his throat while Bala looked on sorrowfully.

When Bookasura had finished, Bala said, 'I will bring more books tomorrow.'

Bookasura disappeared as suddenly as he had come.

Bala slept fitfully that night.

Another Encounter with Bookasura

The next day Ambu Paati was taken aback when Bala said he was going to Navaneeth uncle's house again. 'But you said you saw a monster. You were so frightened. Why do you want to go there again?'

'You were right, there is no monster. I'm sure I imagined it.' Bala had to convince them there was no monster. Otherwise they would not let him go. He *had* to go to Navaneeth uncle's house. He had promised Bookasura he would bring him three books every day. 'I was tired, I must have dozed off. It must have been a dream.'

'I'm glad you saw sense finally,' was Raghu Thaatha's response.

Bala said nothing. He carried his bag. There were just three books left now. Even those would be gone today. Then he would be left with none. What would he do then? How would he feed Bookasura? Bala decided to worry about that later. For today, he had three books. He had to find a way to get them to Bookasura.

Raghu Thaatha dropped Bala off at Navaneeth uncle's house.

'You're here again?' Kala aunty looked Bala up and down.

'I'm feeling fine today. Are you ready to get your hands dirty?' Navaneeth uncle said cheerfully.

Bala nodded.

'Good, let's get started then. Lots of work to be done!' Navaneeth uncle started off.

'Remember ... not near the well,' Kala aunty looked at Bala suspiciously.

They spent the next couple of hours digging a compost pit and filling it up with kitchen and garden waste. When they were done, Bala covered it with soil.

It was time to meet Bookasura and hand him the books. But Navaneeth uncle wanted to clean the fish pond next.

Bala tried to do it as quickly as possible. By the time they had finished, it was late.

'Run off now and find some fruits. Treat yourself to whatever you like,' Navaneeth uncle said.

Bala rushed, but not to find fruits for himself. He headed towards the well. It was growing dark. He could hear the frogs and crickets. He ran past the jackfruit, mango, guava and lemon trees. Finally, he was at the clearing beyond which were the coconut trees. He had reached the well.

Bookasura was waiting outside his cave.

'You are late.' Bookasura sounded subdued, not as ferocious as before.

'Whatever you gave me yesterday didn't agree with my tummy. I'm wary of mice and little boys now. Today's fare better be good,' Bookasura said. He was definitely milder. He wasn't baring his fangs. There had been no lightning or thunder either. Bala felt brave.

'I'm very hungry!' Bookasura was drooling.

'*The Very Hungry Caterpillar*,' Bala said.

'I'm not a caterpillar. Do you think I am a worm? What do you think I am?' Bookasura gnashed his teeth at Bala.

'*Cave Baby*,' Bala said.

'You called me a baby?' Bookasura snarled.

'*Scaredy Squirrel*,' said Bala.

Bookasura was frothing at every mouth by now.

'I brought you three books—*The Very Hungry Caterpillar, Cave Baby* and *Scaredy Squirrel*,' Bala handed over the books.

Bookasura licked his lips and proceeded to eat the books. When he was done, he let out a loud belch.

Bookasura was back to his vicious old self. 'That was good. Bring me more such books. No more stories in which little creatures defeat monsters. Do you understand?' Bookasura bellowed.

Bala nodded obediently and walked back deep in thought.

***

'No monsters today, eh?' Raghu Thaatha was waiting for Bala. Bala said nothing.

'He did a lot of work in the garden,' Navaneeth uncle looked at Bala fondly.

Raghu Thaatha seemed happy to hear that. They left for home.

The Plan

That night Bala could not sleep. He lay in bed staring at the ceiling and watching the fan whir.

Bala was terrified. He did not have any more books. He had promised to bring Bookasura three books every day. What would happen if he did not? Bookasura was sure to eat him. What was Bala going to do? He was desperate. He had to save his own life. But how? How was he going to save himself?

Bala thought of all the books in which small creatures had outwitted fearsome monsters. *The Gruffalo* ... The mouse had used his wits to scare the fox, the owl and even the Gruffalo! *Where the*

Wild Things Are ... Max had been crowned king of all the wild things just by looking them in the eye. Bala couldn't do that—Bookasura had the sun and moon as eyes, and Appa said one must never look directly at the sun. So Bala couldn't do what Max had done, but maybe he could do something

like that! He was definitely going to try. He just needed a good idea.

Bala thought hard. Everyone said he was full of ideas and that it came from reading. Amma said books fed imagination, while TV killed it. She made TV sound like a mighty weapon.

That's when it struck him! He had a weapon!

Bala had a plan. Now he could go to sleep in peace.

The next morning, Bala woke up with a smile. He spent the day eating, listening to stories and pottering about at home.

In the evening, Bala pretended to have a headache when Raghu Thaatha asked about going to Navaneeth uncle's house. Ambu Paati was concerned, but Bala brushed it off. Finally, Paati and Thaatha left for the temple.

Bala was all alone at home.

Bala versus Bookasura

Bala knew Bookasura would come after him when he did not deliver the books. He lay in wait for Bookasura.

In the silence, Bala could hear his heart beat. It thumped so loud, Bala thought it would explode. With great difficulty, he calmed himself. It was so quiet, it was eerie.

Then, he heard the all-too-familiar sounds. There was a flash of lightning, then thunder.

'Where have you been?' came the booming voice.

Bookasura appeared in Bala's room. He was in a rage.

'Where are the books you promised? You

better have them or I will make you my meal,'
Bookasura said menacingly.

'Don't be angry. I have a surprise treat for you
today,' Bala said calmly.

'Hurry up! I'm famished. It's way past my mealtime.'

Bala switched on the TV. *Chhota Bheem* appeared on screen.

Chhota Bheem was everyone's favourite cartoon character at school. He was just as big as Bala,

but extraordinarily strong, just like Bhima. And he had so many exciting adventures!

Bookasura was sprawled on the sofa, watching TV. His face was getting redder. In a few minutes, his face turned a beetroot red and he had bloodshot eyes. He cried out, 'Spare me! Don't torture me! I can't take it anymore! Stop this! Take it away!'

Bala didn't move.

'Do something! I'm getting blinded.' Bookasura covered his eyes and groaned.

Bookasura was going all strange. There was smoke coming out of his ears and nostrils. He held the sides of his heads and moaned. His eyeballs fell onto the floor!

Then his heads split open, all of them. Gooey lumps came squishing out. It was like the cauliflower curry his mother made, except that it had a foul stench. There were worms wriggling all over the soft rotting parts of Bookasura's brains. The wires which held them together were rusted and giving way. Something small and black and round like goat droppings lay right in the middle. It heaved and gasped and quivered, and finally stopped breathing. Bala said a silent prayer for Bookasura's imagination.

Bookasura's body shook and shivered all over. It seemed to be growing bigger.

Yes, it was definitely puffing up ... ballooning ... Bala was afraid Bookasura would burst!

Great clouds of steam poured out. Bookasura

whistled like a pressure cooker. The whistle turned into a roar. Bookasura erupted like a volcano. He clutched his stomach and lurched forward, throwing up all the books he had ever eaten, millions of them from each mouth.

Then one head bounced onto the floor. And another. And another. One by one, they fell onto the floor, bouncing around like basketballs. They slowed down and finally stopped, lying motionless on the ground.

The monster was now headless and harmless. He could eat neither Bala nor his books now. Bala moved aside to let him pass. Bookasura stumbled into the darkness. The TV had zapped his eyes and brains and body. Bhima had defeated Bakasura, and *Chhota Bheem* had helped Bala overcome Bookasura.

Bala looked at the mushy mangled mass lying below him on the ground. What a mess! Then he looked beyond it, at the books Bookasura had spewed out. There were so many of them. Where was he going to keep all those books? What if Baby ate the pages?

Bala pulled at the hair near his ears. Idea! Bala

ran after Bookasura shouting, 'All those books you spat out? I'm going to set up a library with them! I'll read to you every day. It'll be fun!'

Every day, Bala picked three books and set off for the cave. Bala sat outside the cave reading to Bookasura. Every single day, by the end of the third story, Bala would hear Bookasura snoring peacefully.

***

If you happen to be in Melagam in summer, you might find Bala reading to Bookasura.

Bala's books eaten by Bookasura:-

 I Can Read with My Eyes Shut! by Dr. Seuss

 No, David! by David Shannon

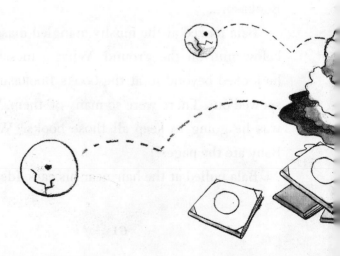

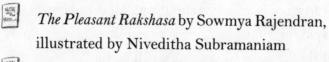

ABOUT THE AUTHOR

Arundhati Venkatesh has always been making up stories. Now she puts them down on paper. She believes fantasy and reality are different ways of looking at the same thing. Books, riddles, magic and *murukku* are a few of her favourite things. When she is not cooking up stories or dreaming of food, she haunts bookstores and libraries in Bangalore.

Her books, *Junior Kumbhakarna, Petu Pumpkin: Tiffin Thief and Petu Pumpkin: Tooth Troubles* were published in 2014.

You can write to her at author.arundhati@gmail.com and find out more about her at arundhativenkatesh.wordpress.com.

ABOUT THE ILLUSTRATOR

Priya Kuriyan is a children's book illustrator, comic book artist and an animator. Born in Cochin, she grew up in numerous towns in India. A graduate of the National Institute of Design, she has directed educational films for the Sesame street show (India) and the Children's Film Society of India (CFSI). She currently lives and works in New Delhi, and makes funny caricatures of its residents in her sketch books.